Who Wears...

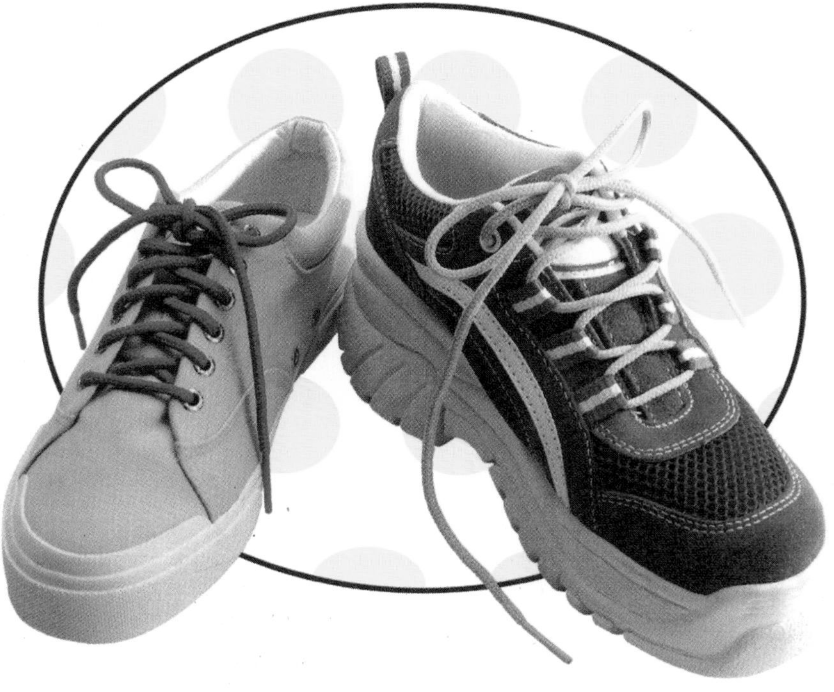

Written by Iris Zammit
Photographs by John Paul Endress

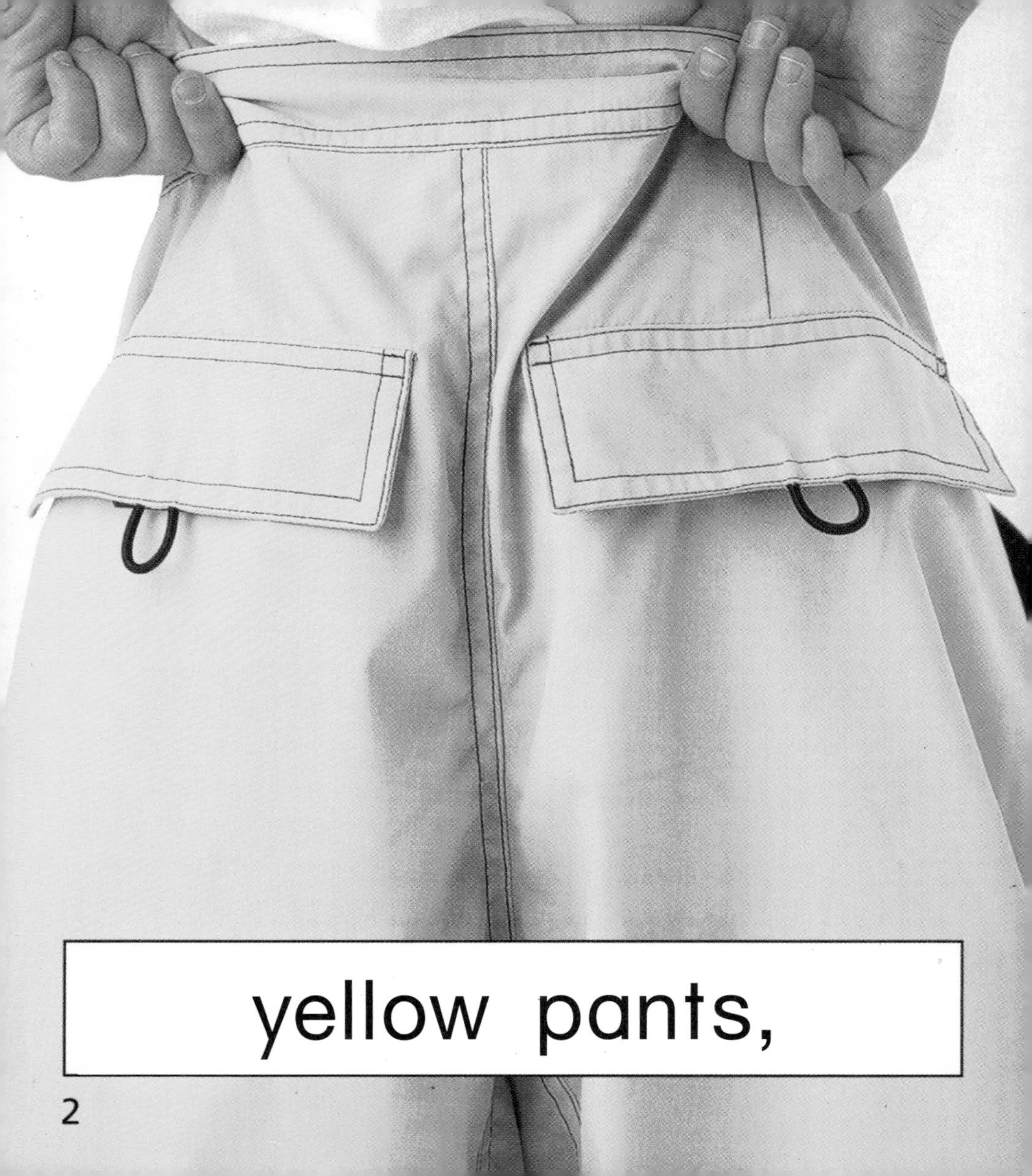

yellow pants,

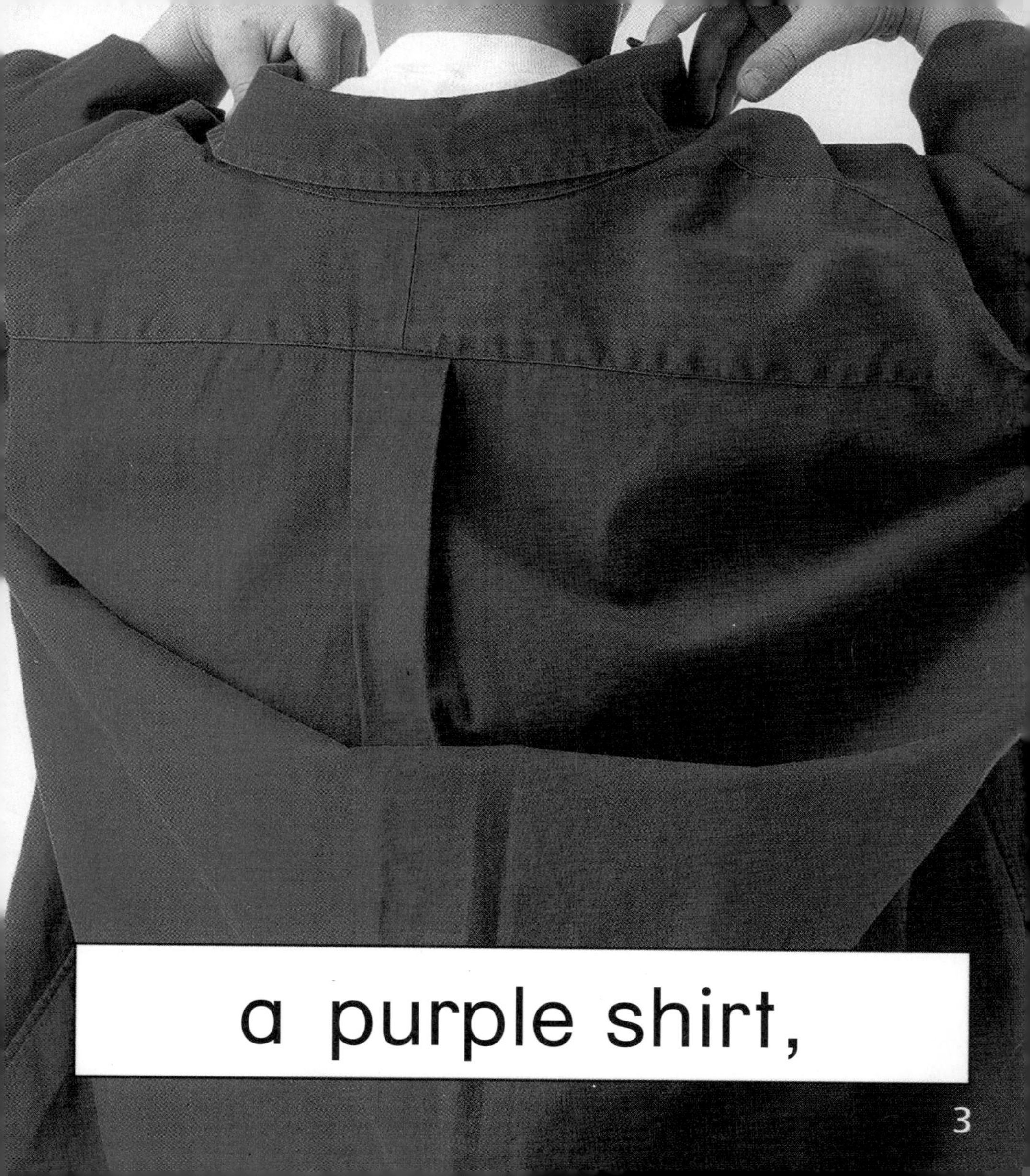

a purple shirt,

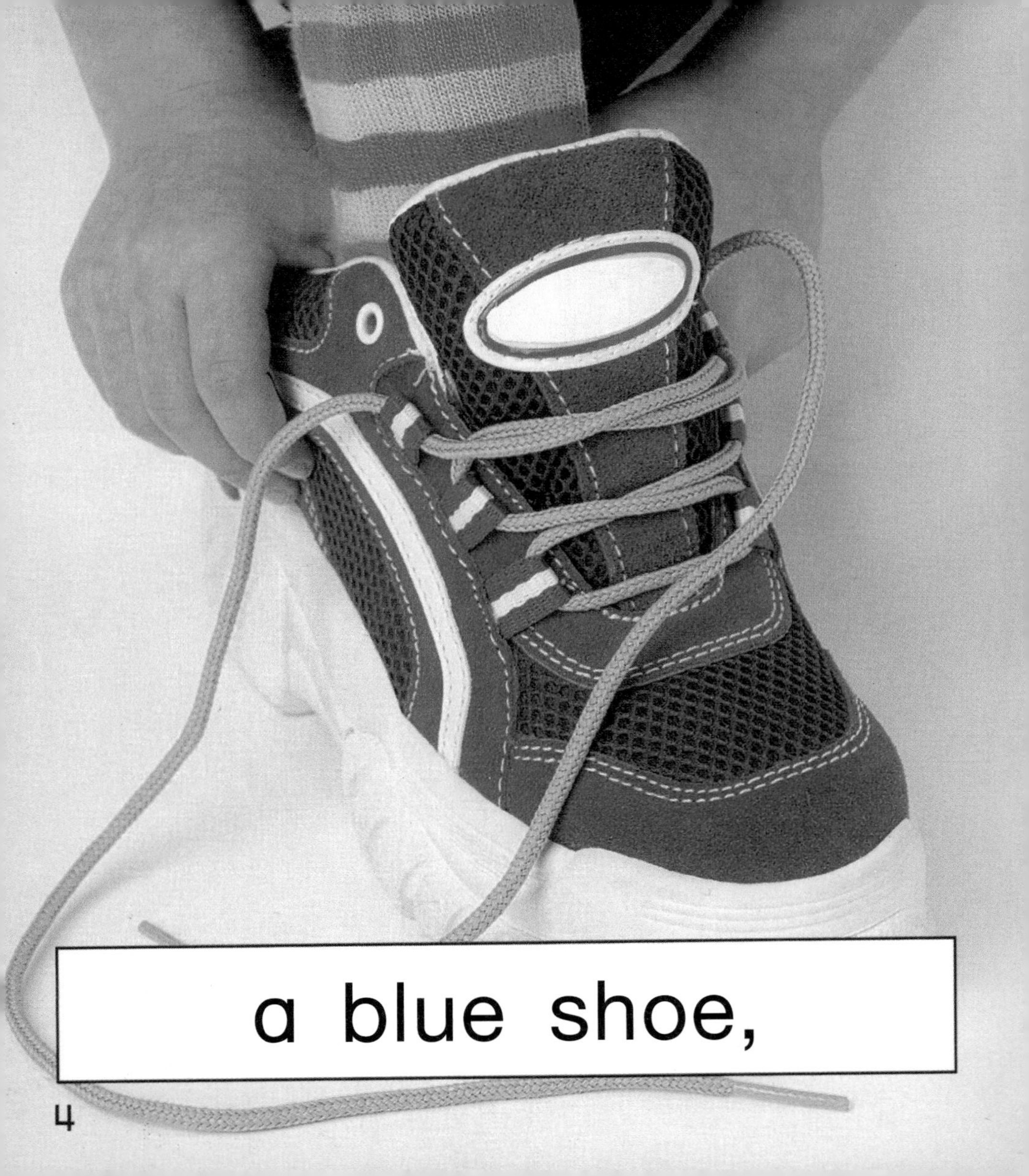

a blue shoe,

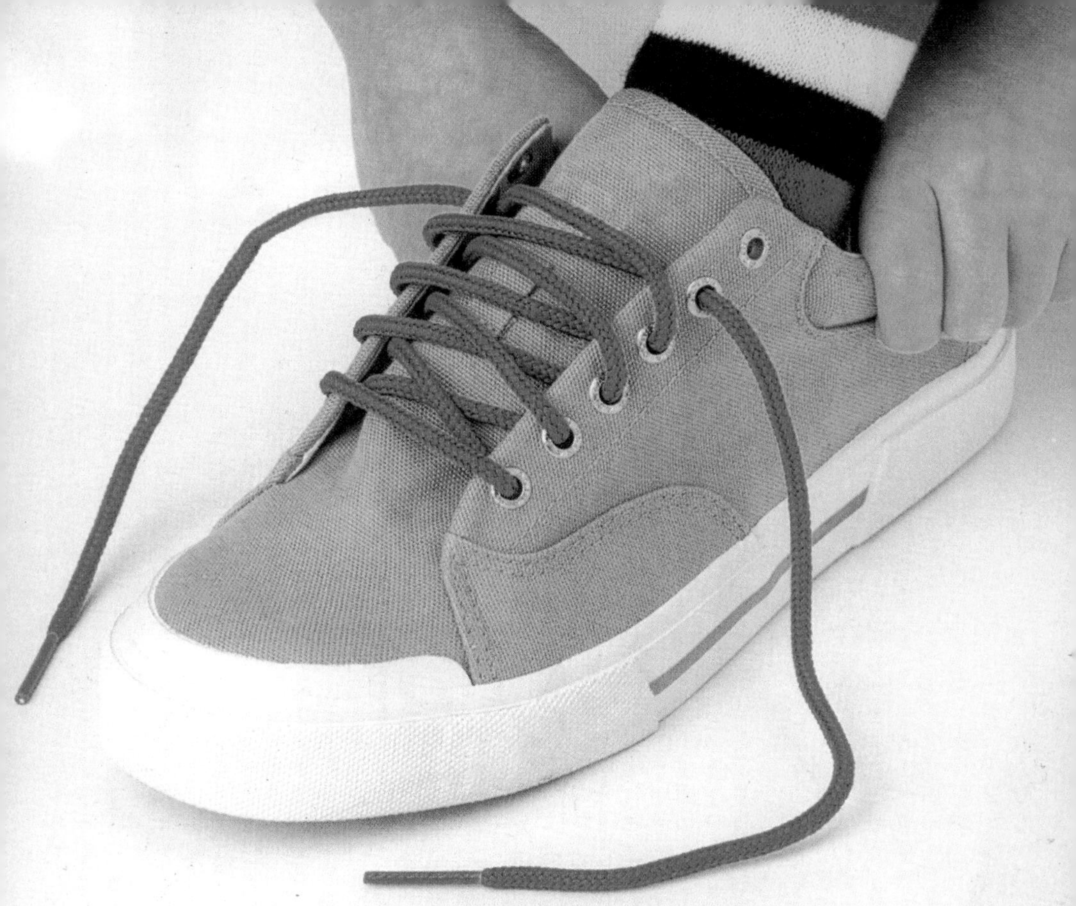

a green shoe,

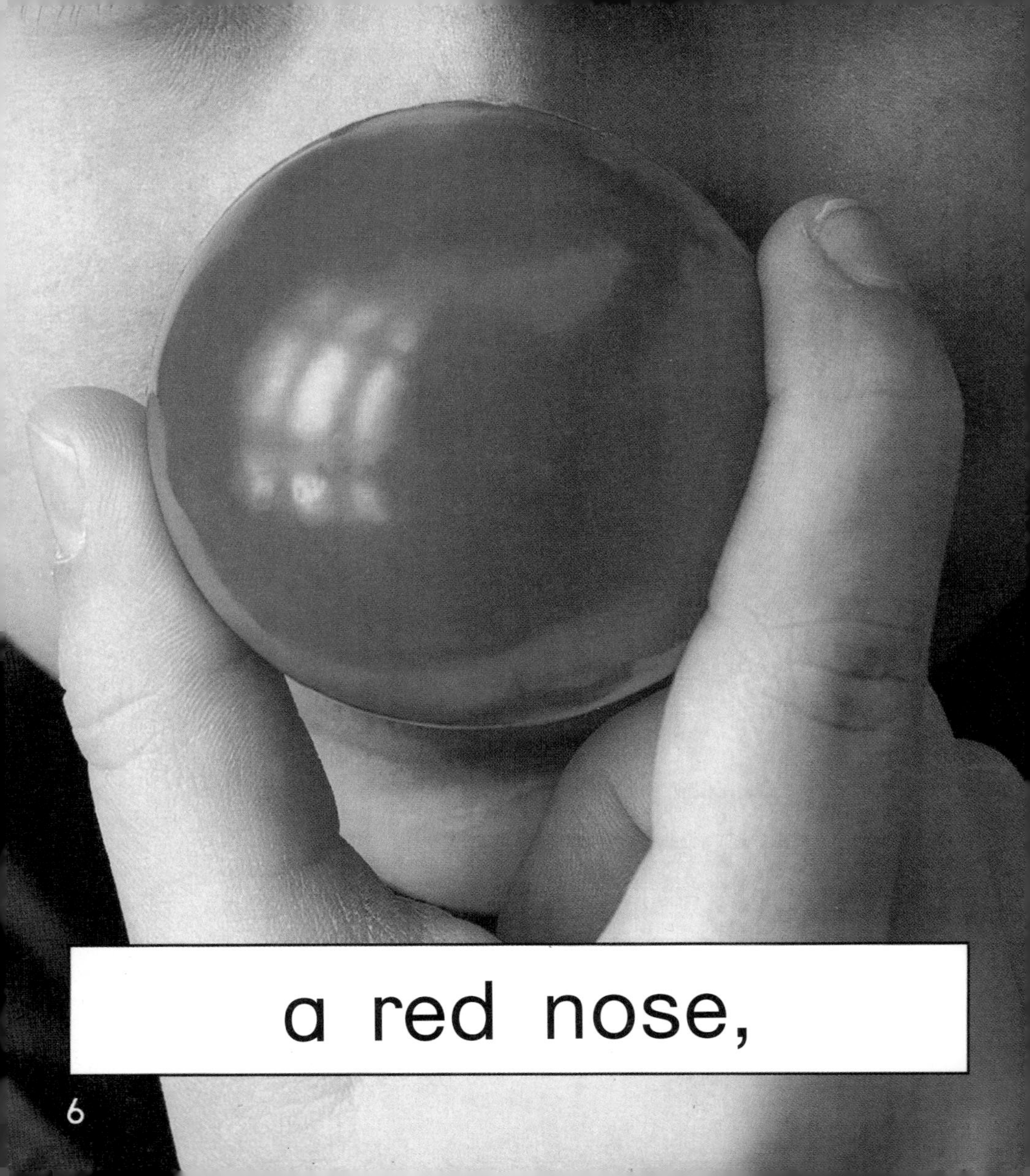

a red nose,

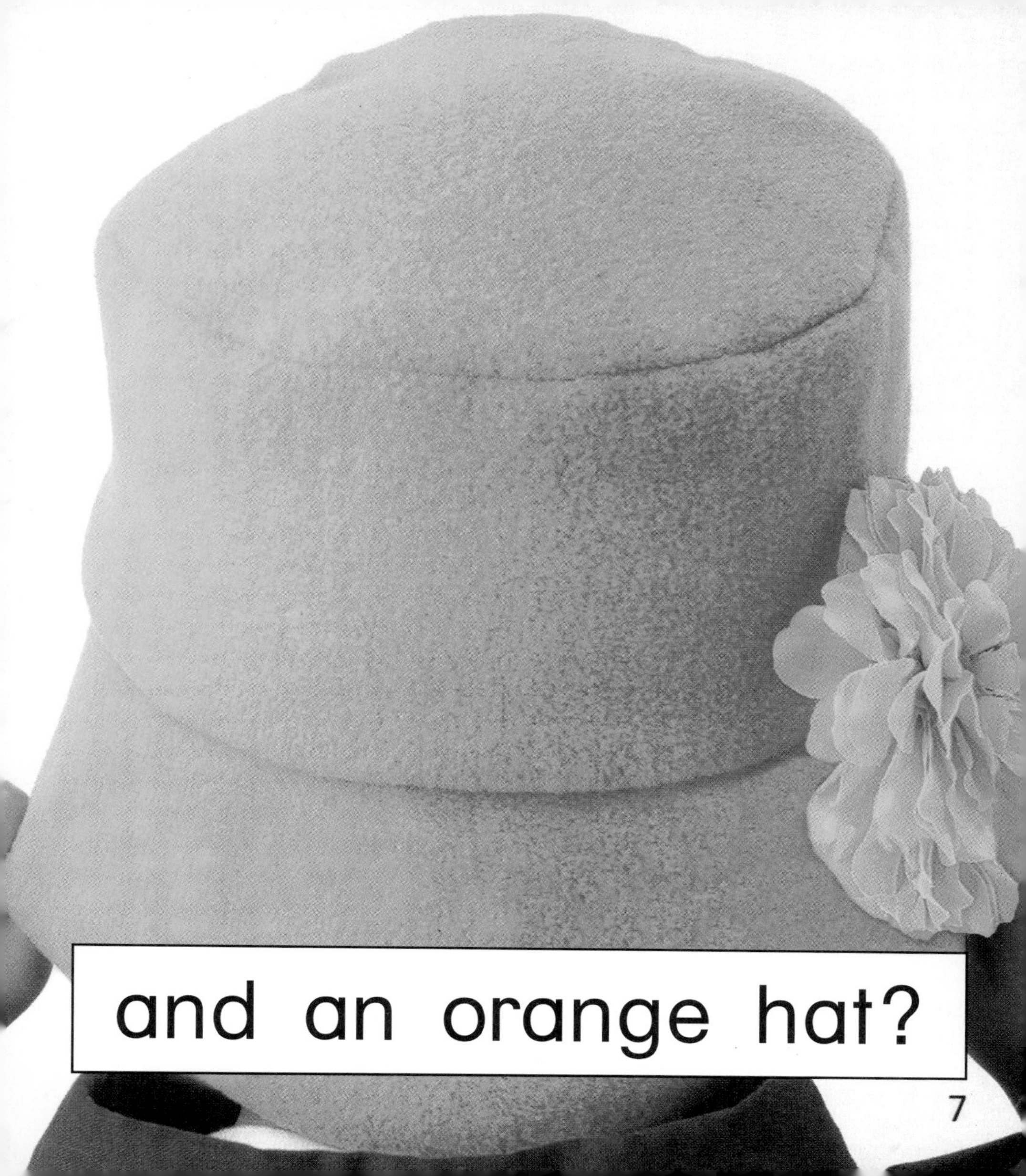

and an orange hat?

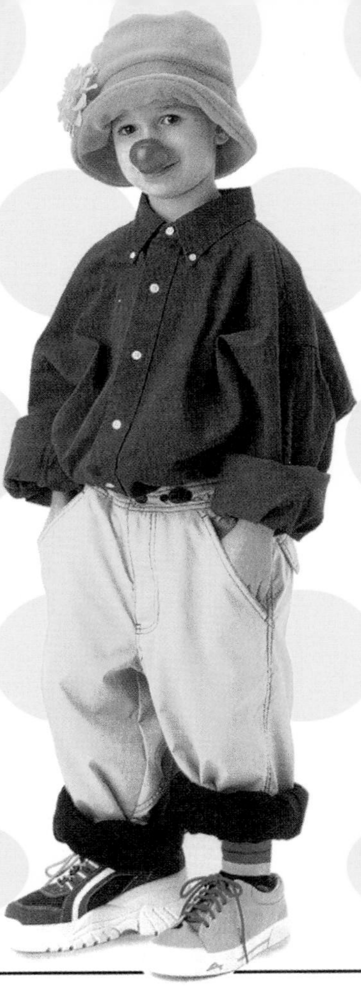

Me!